Gregory, the Terrible Eater

by Mitchell Sharmat

illustrated by Jose Aruego and Ariane Dewey

Four Winds Press New York

Text copyright © 1980 by Mitchell Sharmat. Illustrations copyright © 1980 by José Aruego & Ariane Dewey. All rights reserved.

ISBN 0-590-40250-1

For Andrew, and the goat who tried to eat his coat

Once there was a goat named Gregory.

Gregory liked to jump from rock to rock, kick his legs into the air, and butt his head against walls.

"I'm an average goat," said Gregory.

But Gregory was not an average goat.
Gregory was a terrible eater.
Every time he sat down to eat with his mother and father, he knew he was in for trouble.

"Would you like a tin can, Gregory?" asked Mother Goat.

"No, thanks," said Gregory.

"How about a nice box, a piece of rug, and a bottle cap?" asked Father Goat.

"Baaaaaa," said Gregory unhappily.

"Well, I think this is a meal fit for a goat," said Mother Goat, as she chewed on an old shoe.

"It certainly is," said Father Goat, as he ate a shirt, buttons and all. "I don't know why you're such a fussy eater, Gregory."

"I'm not fussy," said Gregory. "I just want fruits, vegetables, eggs, fish, bread, and butter. Good stuff like that."

Mother Goat stopped eating the shoe. "Now what kind of food is *that*, Gregory?" she said.

"It's what I like," said Gregory.

"It's revolting," said Father Goat. He wiped his mouth with his napkin.

After Gregory was excused from the table, Father Goat said, "Gregory is such a terrible eater."

"I wonder what's wrong with him," said Mother Goat.

Mother and Father Goat ate their evening newspaper in silence.

The next morning Mother and Father Goat were enjoying a pair of pants and a coat for breakfast.

Gregory came to the table.

"Good morning, Gregory," said Father and Mother Goat.

"Good morning," said Gregory. "May I have some orange juice, cereal, and bananas for breakfast, please."

"Oh, no!" Mother Goat said. "Do have some of this nice coat."
"Take a bite out of these pants," said Father Goat.
"Baaaaaa," said Gregory. And he left the table.
Father Goat threw down his napkin. "That does it!" he said.
"Gregory just isn't eating right. We must take him to the doctor."

Father and Mother Goat took Gregory to the doctor.
Dr. Ram was munching on a few pieces of cardboard.

"What seems to be the trouble?" he asked.

"Gregory is a terrible eater," said Mother Goat. "We've offered him the best—shoes, boxes, magazines, tin cans, coats, pants. But all he wants are fruits, vegetables, eggs, fish, orange juice, and other horrible things."

"What do you have to say about all of this, Gregory?" asked Dr. Ram.

"I want what I like," said Gregory.

"Makes sense," said Dr. Ram. He turned to Mother and Father Goat. "I've treated picky eaters before," he said. "They have to develop a taste for good food slowly. Try giving Gregory one new food each day until he eats everything."

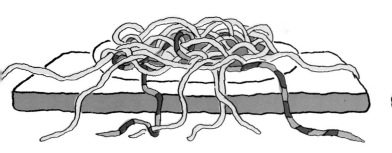 

That night for dinner Mother Goat gave Gregory spaghetti and a shoelace in tomato sauce.

"Not too bad," said Gregory.

The next day she gave him string beans and a rubber heel cut into small pieces.

"The meal was good and rubbery," said Gregory.

The day after that, Mother Goat said, "We have your favorite today. Vegetable soup. But there is one condition. You also have to eat the can."

"Okay," said Gregory. "What's for dessert?"

"Ice cream," said Father Goat. "But you have to eat the box, too."

"Yummy," said Gregory.

"I'm proud of you," said Father Goat. "You're beginning to eat like a goat."

"I'm learning to like everything," said Gregory.

One evening Father Goat asked, "Has anyone seen my striped necktie?"

"Not since breakfast," said Mother Goat. "Come to think of it, I haven't seen my sewing basket today. I left it in the living room after supper last night."

Father Goat turned to Gregory. "Gregory, have you been eating between meals?"

"Yes," said Gregory. "I can't help it. Now I like everything."

"Well," said Mother Goat, "it's all right to eat like a goat, but you shouldn't eat like a pig."

"Oh," said Gregory.

After Gregory went to bed, Mother Goat said, "I'm afraid Gregory will eat my clothes hamper."

"Yes, and then my tool kit will be next," said Father Goat. "He's eating too much. We'll have to do something about it."

The next evening, just before supper, Mother and Father Goat went to the town dump.

They brought home eight flat tires, a three-foot piece of barber pole, a broken violin, and half a car. They piled everything in front of Gregory's sandbox.

When Gregory came home for supper he said, "What's all that stuff in the yard?"

"Your supper," said Father Goat.

"It all looks good," said Gregory.

Gregory ate the tires and the violin. Then he slowly ate the barber pole. But when he started in on the car, he said, "I've got a stomachache. I have to lie down."

Gregory went to his room.
"I think Gregory ate too much junk," said Father Goat.
"Let's hope so," said Mother Goat.

All night Gregory tossed and twisted and moaned and groaned.

The next morning he went down for breakfast.

"What would you like for breakfast today, Gregory?" asked Father Goat.

"Scrambled eggs and two pieces of waxed paper and a glass of orange juice," said Gregory.

"That sounds just about right," said Mother Goat.

And it was.

Fun-To-Do Activities Begin on Page 50

Behind the Scenes

Introduction

All parents want their babies to eat well. In *Gregory, the Terrible Eater,* Father Goat and Mother Goat teach Gregory to like foods that will help him to grow into a healthy, happy goat. Baby animals grow up in many different ways. Each kind needs its own special food, home and care.

Loads of Goats

Baby goats are called *kids* — but they're not like people kids! A kid goat can stand and walk without wobbling on the same day it is born. It may even try to climb down stairs! Goats are fast and sure-footed. It's hard to trip a goat. They love to run and jump and climb rocks.

Mother goats usually have *twins*. Twins are two babies born at the same time. Some goats have horns, some do not. It all depends on what kind of goat it is. If a baby goat is going to have horns, tiny buds can be felt on its head.

Most farm goats are usually raised for milking. Some human babies get sick on cow's milk. Goat's milk is often better for them. It is rich in minerals and sweeter than cow's milk. Many kinds of cheeses are made from goat's milk, too.

Goats eat hay, alfalfa, oats, corn and apples. Goats are not at all shy. They love to chew on shirttails, belt straps and straw hats. If you hear that goats eat tin cans, don't believe it. They pull paper labels off cans because they like the taste of the glue used to attach the labels to the cans.

Goats are very lively and curious. They are so adventurous that their mothers never have to nudge them out into the world. Getting them to come back home can be difficult, in fact.

Rabbits

A baby rabbit is called a *kitten*. Its mother is called a *doe*. The father is called a *buck*. The kittens are born in an underground burrow called a *warren*. The doe makes a nest for her babies. The nest is made of grass and soft fur the doe pulls from her stomach.

The baby rabbits feed on their mother's milk when they're born. When kittens are two weeks old, they begin to eat solid food. They eat green leafy plants like clover and marigold in the summer. In the winter they eat twigs and tree bark. After six weeks, the baby rabbits must survive on their own. But before the doe lets them go, she trains them to run from danger—humans, other ground animals and birds. By then, the mother is often ready to have another litter of kittens.

Behind the Scenes

Cows

Most baby animals are helpless at birth, but a baby cow, or *calf*, can stand up thirty minutes after being born. A calf will look for its mother and her milk first. The calf feeds at its mother's *udder*. An udder looks like a bag and hangs underneath the cow. The calf drinks only mother's

milk for the first four days. Then it feeds on hay and grain. *Hay* is dried grasses, clover and other plants. *Grain* is the seeds of plants like wheat and oats. When a calf is one year old, it is called a *heifer*. It is turned out to pasture with the grown-up cows and is on its own from then on.

Baby Baboons

Baby baboons are often born during the rainy season. The grasses that grow during the rainy season help the mother and the baby baboons. For two weeks the baby just clings to its mother's stomach. Slowly it tries out the ground a few minutes at a time until it's comfortable. Baby baboons look different than their parents. They have pink faces, not dark ones; and they have black hair, not brown. A baboon family is called a *troop*. All the grownups in the troop love to play with the babies.

Although the little baboon drinks mother's milk for its first four months, it soon learns to try adult food. At first a baboon imitates its mother by pulling up grasses. But it doesn't taste them. Next, a baboon tastes, but doesn't swallow the grasses. Baboons travel to eat. They go where the tallest and sweetest grasses are growing. They often go as far as three or four miles from home for food. When the troop travels, a big male baboon leads. Mothers and babies stay in the center where they are safe from enemies.

At six months old, the baby baboons in the troop are playing monkey games that look like "Follow the Leader" and "King of the Castle." At about this age the baby baboon learns to ride on its mother's back. It

has a better view of the world from up there. Now, too, its face begins to get darker and its hair lighter. At seven months it will begin to eat grasses for survival. But a baby baboon often continues to drink milk until it's ten months old.

The little baboon will not be fully grown until it is three-and-a-half or four years old. By the end of a baboon's first year, its mother will probably be nursing a new baby brother or sister.

Garbage—Here Today, Gone Tomorrow

There's magic in garbage. Somehow it disappears every day. Do you know how? Or where it goes? Here's the inside story.

The trucks that pick up garbage from your house or apartment go to a building where the garbage is weighed. Each city keeps track of how

many tons it collects each day. This figure tells the city if and when it needs more garbage collectors or trucks.

Much of the garbage that is collected is burned. Sometimes it is burned at the weighing building, a place called a sanitation terminal. Often it is shipped to an incinerator near a landfill. An *incinerator* is a furnace used for burning trash, reducing it to ashes. A *landfill* is an area where garbage is dumped, flattened by bulldozers, and then covered with earth every day. This gets rid of the garbage and adds new land for the city or town to build on someday. You'd be surprised how many buildings are built on landfill. Do you know of any in your own town?

Use It Again

Other kinds of trash do not have to be burned or buried. They can be used again. And again, and again. This is called *recycling*.

Junk cars, for instance, are sometimes flattened into cubes of scrap metal. The car's engine is melted down for reuse as new automobile parts.

Behind the Scenes

What's left from the junk metal cube can be mixed in concrete. This concrete can be made into strong blocks for building bridge supports and thick walls.

Airplanes can also be recycled. Planes still able to fly may have second lives as fire-fighting planes, in taking photos from the air, and advertising in the air. Some planes are sold for scrap after all the useful parts have been sold. If a plane is too old to fly well, it is cut into pieces and melted down into an aluminum cube. Then the aluminum can be used in another plane, car or even a frying pan.

A more familiar recycled product is paper. Burning paper makes the air dirty, and there's not enough room to bury all our waste paper. So using it again is the best way to get rid of it. Old paper can be reused to make newsprint, cardboard cartons, brown bag paper or greeting cards.

Recycling paper helps save our trees, too. How? For every *ton* (2000 lbs.) of paper recycled, 17 trees stay alive. Check the brown bags from the supermarket, and look at the backs of greeting cards—these things often say that they're made from recycled paper. In the United States, we waste 428,570,000 (that's millions!) pounds of paper every day. That translates into 3½ million trees worth of paper. So you might want to think twice about how much paper *you* waste.

You Can Help

Bottles and cans can be recycled, too. Many communities have recycling centers where families can take them. From these centers old cans and bottles are sent to manufacturers who will process the glass and aluminum for reuse. Some centers pay people for paper products, bottles and cans they bring; some do not. In any case, recycling centers are a fine way to get rid of garbage and make sure we are making the best use of what nature provides us.

Garbage Art

Some things are not recycled into *products* (or things that we use). They appear again — as art. An artist can look at trash and see unusual and unexpected beauty. You can find examples of this kind of art in many places around the country.

Just outside Los Angeles, California, stand three famous towers. They are made of cement but decorated with bits of colored glass, broken pottery, junk metal, shells and wire. From a distance they look like towers of metal lace.

Watts Towers,
Los Angeles,
California

In Amarillo, Texas, there's an acre of land called Cadillac Ranch. Three artists half-buried ten old Cadillac cars, hood down, in the rich land. People come from all over the country to see this strange sight.

Outside the Children's Museum in Detroit, Michigan, stands an eight-foot horse sculpture. It is made entirely of automobile bumpers from a scrap yard. Many cars have been made in Detroit, so this sculpture has a special meaning to the city whose cars replaced the horse on American roads.

Horse sculpture, Detroit, Michigan

Perhaps there are beautiful things in your own home made from recycled garbage. How about that patchwork quilt on your bed? Who was it who took those pretty scraps of cloth and saw the lovely quilt waiting to be made from them? Or the knee patches on your jeans? Before you throw anything away, why not think about other ways it could be used?

Behind the Scenes

A Doctor's Office

When you visit a doctor's office, you'll find many things that you find nowhere else. Here are some of them. Have you seen these already? Have you ever wondered what they were? Next time you have a check-up, impress your doctor with all these new words.

An *eye chart* is usually on the wall in the room where you are examined. The doctor will ask you to read the letters on the eye chart. Each line of letters is smaller than the one above it. Some of the letters may face in different directions. The doctor uses an eye chart to check your eyesight.

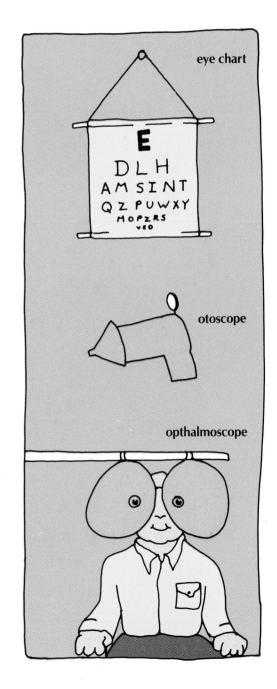

eye chart

otoscope

opthalmoscope

The *otoscope* (say: **ah**-toe-scope) is a small, strong flashlight with a magnifying glass. It is used to look inside the small holes in your ears and nose.

The *opthalmoscope* (say: ahp-**thal**-muh-scope) is another instrument the doctor uses. It shines a light into your eye. The doctor can then see the inside of your eye and make sure it looks healthy. The doctor will tell you to look straight ahead, maybe at a place on the wall — hard to do with the light shining in your eyes!

A *tongue depressor* is a flat stick. The doctor presses it on your tongue to make it easier to check your throat and tonsils for signs of trouble.

The *stethoscope* (say: **steth**-uh-scope) is like a microscope for heart and lung sounds. The two branches of this instrument go into the doctor's ears. The bottom part, a little horn-shaped piece, goes against your chest. This is how the doctor listens to the sounds of your heart and lungs. Take a deep breath, the doctor will say. Deeper. Okay, exhale.

A small *hammer* with a rubber tip is used to test your reflexes. A reflex is a movement your body makes without your thinking about it. The doctor taps your knees and elbows with the hammer. These reflexes are another way of checking to see that everything is fine.

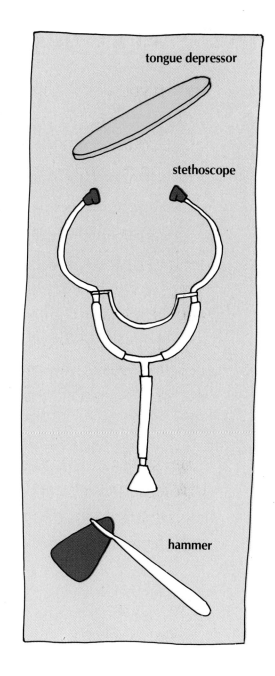

tongue depressor

stethoscope

hammer

Say Aah!

Do you go to the doctor for a check-up every year? If so, this pen pal letter about visiting a new doctor will sound familiar. Is your doctor the same? Or different? In what ways?

Behind the Scenes

Dear Pal

I like this new town a lot, but I miss you. Do you miss me too?

Mom took me to visit the doctor here yesterday. Her office is downtown near City Hall. Mom and I waited in a room with some other kids and parents. I read a comic book for awhile.

The nurse called my name. The doctor said "hello" and shook my hand. Mom's too. First, I got on a scale. The scale weighed me and measured my height at the same time. Then the doctor asked me to walk up and down the room. She said she was checking to see if my back and legs were straight or needed some help. Special shoes, maybe?

Then she put me up on a table and asked if I'd had measles, mumps or chicken pox yet. Mom told the doctor all the details and the nurse wrote them on my chart.

Next the doctor looked in my ears with a light and down my throat with a stick while I said "aah." She shined the light in my eyes too. The doctor told me brown eyes were her favorite and Mom laughed. Hers are green.

On our way out Mom made an appointment with the nurse. I have to go back and visit the doctor again in six months. She was real nice, so I don't mind.

Love, Your friend

P.S. I got a chart to measure my height each month, too!

What You Eat

Every day you do things that keep you healthy. You get enough sleep. You brush your teeth. You keep your body clean. You eat good food. But eating good food doesn't come as naturally as the others. That's where nutrition comes in. *Nutrition* is about feeding a body what it needs to stay well.

There are three types of foods that the body needs. The three are *carbohydrates* (say: car-bo-**hi**-drates), *proteins* and *fats*. Most foods are mixtures of two or even all three groups. But meat, fish and poultry are mostly protein. Breads, cereals and rice are common carbohydrate sources. Fats are found in salad oils, butter, nuts and seeds. The proper balance of all three is the basis of good nutrition.

Proteins are the building materials in your body. As you grow, you need more of them than an adult does. But your body doesn't need as much protein as you might think — ½ a hamburger, or 2 slices of Swiss cheese, provides the recommended amount of protein per day.

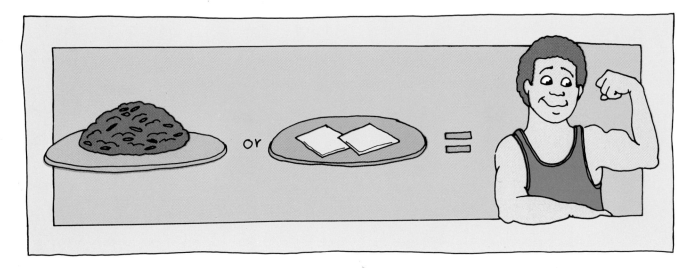

Your body uses carbohydrates and fats for energy. Fats are quick energy but too many of them stored in a body cause you to become overweight. Carbohydrates are a slower-burning fuel. If you have a football game or a track meet coming up, you'll get more useful, longer-lasting energy from spaghetti than you will from a candy bar.

Water is an important addition to your diet that many people ignore. The body needs plenty of water to work smoothly. Water carries food in your blood to the muscles and bones that need it. Then it carries away waste. Did you know that your body is wet all over? 71 percent of your body weight is water. That means that if you weigh 100 pounds, 71 pounds are water and 29 pounds are bones, muscles and other stuff.

The body needs a number of salts, called minerals, too. The kind of salt on your dinner table is one of them. But there are others. Calcium, iron and iodine are a few other kinds of salts that the body must have for good health. Calcium is found in milk and cheese, iron in whole wheat bread and cereals, and iodine in ocean fish and iodized salt.

Vitamins

But even a diet of proteins, carbohydrates, fats, plenty of water, and all the minerals would not be enough to keep you alive and healthy for very long. Something's still missing. Vitamins are substances that work in special ways in your body. For example, Vitamin C helps your body fight germs. It can be found in citrus fruits—oranges, lemons, limes—among other foods.

What you eat is important. It makes a difference in how you look, how well you do in school, and how much energy you have to do the things you like to do. Good nutrition is one of the keys to good health. Don't ignore it.

Did You Know...?

Cows have *four* stomachs. They swallow food without chewing it. First it goes into a special storage stomach. The cow can bring it up and rechew the food (called cud) before it goes on to a second, third, and fourth stomachs for thorough digestion. This is where we get the saying for long thinking—"chewing your cud."

Snakes swallow their food—fish, lizards, small animals—whole. Snakes have very strong stomachs that digest everything.

Birds do not have teeth. They swallow chunks of food. Part of a bird's stomach is called a *gizzard*. In the gizzard the food is ground up. The grinding is helped by stones the bird has swallowed. Only then is the ground food digested.

Activities ➡

Activities

Junkyard Jumble

This junkyard is filled with more than just junk. Look carefully at all the things in the picture and you will find some very tasty treats. Can you find the following fruits?

watermelon, pineapple, grapes, strawberry, banana

Time For a Snack

Here's a special snack that's fun to eat and fun to make. And it will keep you healthy, too.

What You Need:

slices of bread   grapes
peanut butter   raisins
slices of fruit—bananas,   nuts
    apples, melon   coconut

What You Do:

- First spread a slice of bread with peanut butter.
- Next decorate the bread with the other ingredients to make a funny face: coconut makes good hair and a mustache; a banana slice makes a silly nose.

What's New At The Zoo

You're looking at a weird and wacky animal called a walarookey. Can you guess how this mixed-up animal got its name? Study the picture for a minute or two and you will know the answer.

Did you guess? You're looking at the face of a walrus, the body of a kangaroo, and the tail of a donkey. It's a wal-aroo-key!

Use your imagination to dream up some other wacky animals. Get out some paper and try to fill a whole zoo.

Activities

Word Search

Hidden in the maze below are words you've just learned. Do you remember what they mean? The words go across and down. Find the words in the maze and write them on another paper.

ENERGY, RECYCLE, BULLDOZER, GARBAGE, ANIMALS

B	U	L	L	D	O	Z	E	R	E
E	R	A	N	I	M	A	L	S	T
R	L	E	A	M	I	T	C	E	R
G	A	R	B	A	G	E	D	A	E
T	F	O	A	I	T	N	I	N	C
E	R	D	D	I	U	E	L	U	Y
N	S	W	O	A	R	R	O	B	C
E	C	K	C	N	U	G	T	O	L
L	A	N	I	E	O	Y	Z	W	E
K	N	A	N	T	E	L	R	S	T

Recycle Your Trash

Don't throw away that milk carton when you drink the last drop of milk. Turn the carton into an easy-to-make bird feeder that you can hang in your yard or set on the windowsill.

What You Need:
a clean, dry half-gallon or gallon milk carton
scissors
picture wire or heavy twine
a large stapler

What You Do:
1. You will need help from a grownup for the first part of this project. Gently poke the scissors through and carefully cut the sides of the carton. Cut away the centers of two opposite sides.

2. Use the cut-away pieces to make a roof for the feeder. First, close the top of the carton and staple it. Then place one cut-away piece on each side of the closing to shape the roof. Staple the pieces to the top of the carton.

3. Poke a hole in the center of the closing. Loop the wire or twine through the hole. Use this to hang the feeder from a tree. Or, set the feeder on a windowsill.

Activities

4. Fill the feeder with seed for wild birds or bread crumbs mixed with fat trimmed from meat.

5. Watch the birds enjoy your feeder. Do they eat quickly? Do they come back often?

Tricky Tongue Twisters

How many times can you repeat each of these tongue twisters?

Four fat frogs, frying fritters, fiddled ferociously.

A big black bug bit a big black bear.

Make up a tongue twister of your own. The more words that begin with the same letter, the more it will twist your tongue! Once you've mastered it, ask your friends to try it.

Garbage Garden

If you're like Gregory the goat, you love oranges and orange juice too! The next time you eat an orange, don't throw away the seeds. Save them and start an orange plant. Follow these easy steps:

1. Save 6 to 8 seeds for each plant you want to grow.

2. Put the seeds in warm water and let them soak overnight before planting.

3. Plant the seeds in potting soil in a small clay pot and water it just until the soil is wet throughout.

4. Place the pot in a sunny window. When the weather is warm, place the pot outdoors in the sun.

5. Water the plant whenever the soil is dry. In 4 to 6 weeks, green shoots will appear. No oranges will grow, but after awhile you'll have a lovely green plant.

6. Want a whole garbage garden? Try other fruit and vegetable seeds and see what you can get to grow.

Activities

Jokes

Gregory the goat has lots of friends. When they come over to play with him, this is what you hear…

Knock, knock.
> Who's there?

Lionel.
> Lionel who?

Lionel get you in trouble every time.

Knock, knock.
> Who's there?

Harry.
> Harry who?

Harry up or we'll be late.

Knock, knock.
> Who's there?

Dewey.
> Dewey who?

Dewey have to play *this* game again!

Knock, knock.
> Who's there?

Noah.
> Noah who?

Noah anymore good knock-knock jokes?

A Puzzling Matter

If you see a group of cows grazing in a field, you might say, "There's a herd of cows." If you see a group of birds flying across the sky, you might say, "Look at the flock of birds." Herd and flock are common names for groups of animals. But some groups have very unusual names. Do you know what to call a group of lions? A group of geese? Solve the rebus puzzles and you will have the answers. Guess the *first letter* of each object to spell the puzzle words.

Example:

A Group of Birds:

FAN   LIGHTBULB   OWL   CLOCK   KEY

FLOCK

A Group of Lions:

A Group of Geese:

Activities

Pebble Pets You Can Make

Some pets make lots of noise and are hard to care for, but not pebble pets. They make great gifts, too. Make more than one pet so your pebble pet doesn't get lonely.

First, collect small rocks of different shapes. Be sure to collect some flat rocks as well as some round ones. Wash and dry all the rocks before you begin. You will need some bristly pipe cleaners and white glue.

Make a Swan:
1. Place a pipe cleaner under a pebble with a flat bottom.
2. Shape the cleaner tightly around the bottom and sides of the pebble.
3. Twist each end of the cleaner into a head and tail for your pet.
4. Twist another cleaner around the tail to make a three-part tail.

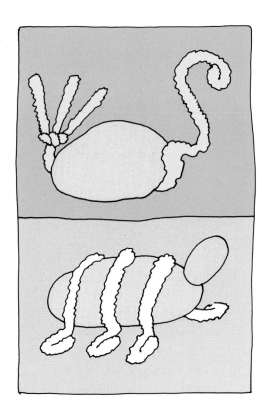

Make a Bug:
1. Shape two or three cleaners around the top of a pebble. Pinch the ends of each cleaner to form little feet.
2. Glue on a smaller pebble to make a head.

You can also make pets from three or four rocks of different sizes glued together. Use your imagination to create a variety of pets. Choose a large rock for the body of the pet and small rocks for the feet and head. Glue on one rock at a time and let it dry before adding another.

A Travel Game

Do you ever get bored on a long car trip? On your next trip, play this game with another person. You won't be bored anymore.

Rules:
1. Memorize the objects listed in one game box.
2. Look for those objects. Call out the name of the object as you see it.
3. On a sheet of paper, write the names of the objects you spot.
4. The first player who spots three of the five objects wins a game.
5. Play games 2 and 3. The person who wins 2 out of 3 games wins a *set*.

You don't have to stop with 3 games. Make up your own list of objects for more games and more fun!

Game 1
Stop sign
trailer truck
pizza truck
4-door black car
gas station

Game 2
Enter sign
yellow traffic light
mail box
ice cream shop
police car

Game 3
doughnut shop
2-door green car
motel
45 MPH sign
Exit sign

Activities

Trivia Game

Trivia are facts that may be unimportant but are very interesting. You can make up a game using trivia. Here are some to start you off. Put them on cards. Write the question on one side and the answer on the other. Stump your friends.

1. Q. Can you name two flowers that people eat?

    A. Broccoli and cauliflower. The top part of each plant is made of many small flowers called florets.

2. Q. What do the sandwich and a card player have in common?

    A. Each other. The sandwich was named after a card player named the Earl of Sandwich. He was an English nobleman who didn't want to stop his card game for meals. The sandwich was invented to hold his meal together so he could eat at the card table.

3. Q. Which bird can fly the farthest, a swallow or an Arctic tern?

    A. An arctic tern makes the longest winter migration trip of any bird. The tern flies from the Arctic at the top of the world to Antarctic at the bottom of the world. That's a trip of about 11,000 miles.

Name The Baby

Everyone knows the name of a baby goat — it's a *kid*. Not everyone knows the name of a baby swan. It's a *cygnet* (say: **sig**-nit). Do you know the names of the baby animals in the pictures below? Unscramble the letters in each word and you'll find the animals' names.

B U C

E T K I N T

Y E O J

N A W F

A L O F

Activities

Get My Goat!

The two look alike, but there are differences. Can you find them?

Sometimes you might hear a person say, "Henry is getting my goat." That means the speaker is very angry with Henry. It also means the speaker is about to "show" his anger!

Paper Bag Puppet

Turn a paper bag into a goat puppet and use it to tell the story of *Gregory, the Terrible Eater* to a friend.

What You Need:

small brown bag   crayon
scissors and glue   scraps of colored paper

What You Do:

1. With the crayon, draw eyes, mouth and a nose on the flap of the bag.

2. Cut ½-inch strips of colored paper for the chin hairs. To curl the strips, run one blade of the scissors across each strip. Glue the strips to the bottom edge of the flap.

3. Follow the patterns to cut shapes for the ears and horns. Glue them to the top edge of the flap. Glue the ears to the front side and the horns to the back side.

4. Put your hand inside the bag. Work the goat's mouth by opening and closing your hand. What is your goat saying?

Activities

Macaroni And...

Uncooked pasta, including macaroni, can be used to make an unusual picture. The more varieties of pasta you use, the better, so see how many you can collect: macaroni, shells, spaghetti, bows, lasagna, ziti and more. You'll need a handful of each to "paint" your picture.

What You Need:

cardboard   glue

pencil   poster paint

different kinds of pasta

What You Do:

1. On the cardboard, outline your picture in pencil.
2. Begin with a small area. Put a thin layer of glue on a section of your picture. Then, lay down pieces of pasta firmly. If you want to make hair, use curly pasta. Macaroni can be used to make waves, or round things.
3. Continue adding glue and then pasta to your picture until it's all filled in. Then, set it aside to dry.
4. When the glue on your pasta picture is dry, add paint. You can paint all the bows red, for example, and all the shells blue, or you can vary the color all over the picture. When the paint is dry, put the picture in your room or give it to someone as a gift.